The P
Babies

Written by Jill Eggleton
Illustrated by Richard Hoit

The possum mother
had twenty babies
in her pouch, but . . .
the babies got **too** big.

The possum mother
couldn't keep them
in her pouch.

The possum babies were
too small to climb trees
like their mother.
They still had to stay
with her.

They held on to her back
and her stomach, and
some held on to her tail.

But there were too many babies.
They couldn't all stay
on their mother.
When their mother
went up the tree,
some babies fell off.

It was dark and
the possum babies
were scared.

They hid under a leaf.

In the morning, the possum babies saw a rabbit by the tree.
So they climbed on to the rabbit.

But the rabbit
didn't have a pouch.
It didn't have a long tail.

When it went hopping
over the grass, the possum
babies fell off.

Then the possum babies
saw a kangaroo.
They saw a long tail.
They saw a big pouch
with just one baby.

The possum babies
climbed on to
the kangaroo's tail.

It was a big tail.
The possum babies
could stay there.

But then the kangaroo jumped.
Her big tail went **thump**
on the ground.

The possum babies
couldn't keep holding on.

Up they went . . .
into the sky and **plonk**
into a tree.

But the possum babies fell . . .
down, down, down!
Then they saw a tail.

And lucky for them . . .
it was their mother's tail.

A Story Sequence

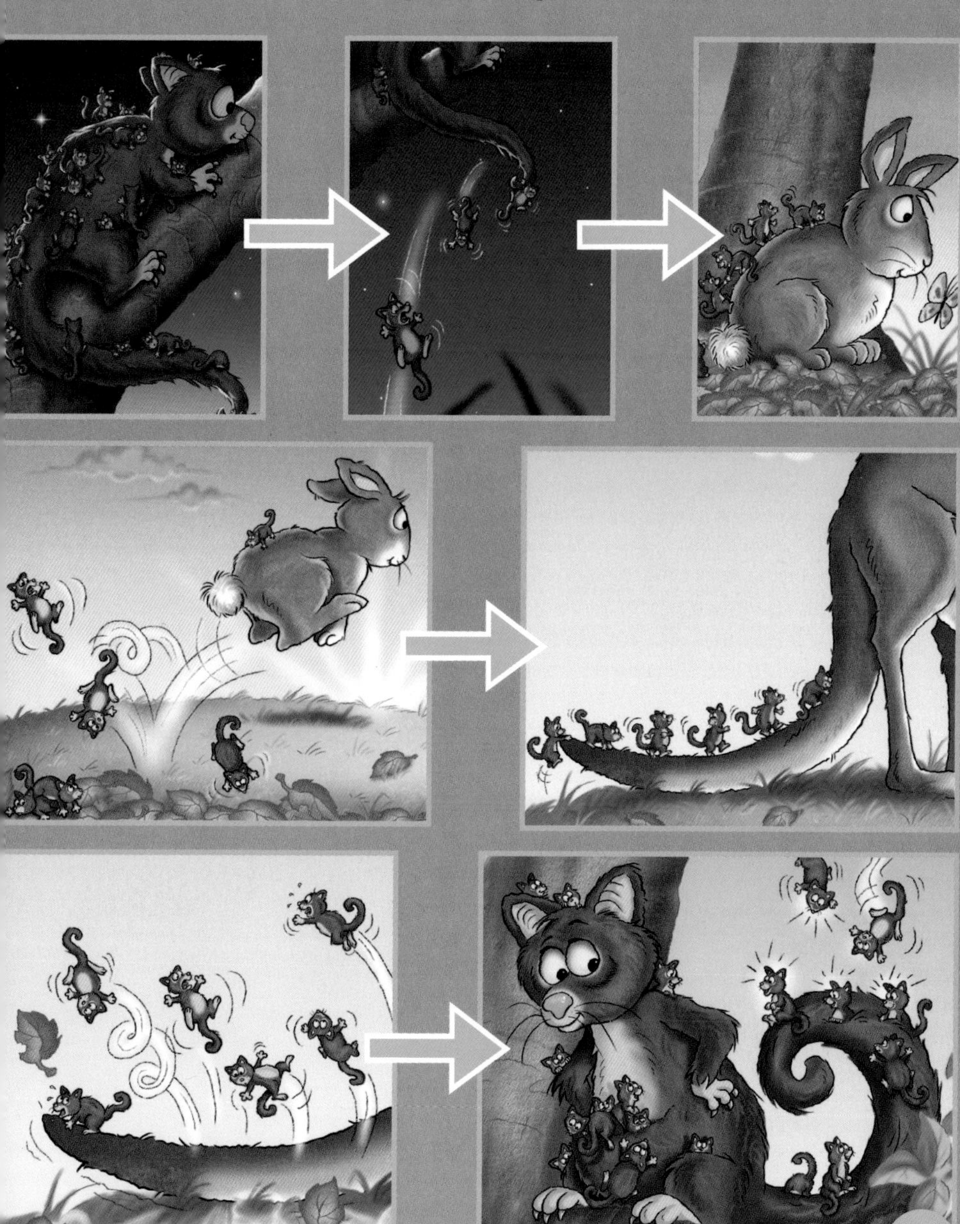

Guide Notes

Title: The Possum Babies
Stage: Early (4) – Green

Genre: Fiction
Approach: Guided Reading
Processes: Thinking Critically, Exploring Language, Processing Information
Written and Visual Focus: Story Sequence

THINKING CRITICALLY

(sample questions)

- What do you think this story could be about? Look at the title and discuss.
- Look at the cover. Why do you think the possum babies are hanging onto their mother?
- Look at pages 2 and 3. Why do you think it is important that the possum babies stay with their mother?
- Look at pages 6 and 7. What do you think could happen to the possum babies if they stayed out in the open?
- Look at pages 8 and 9. Why do you think the possum babies climbed onto the rabbit?
- Look at pages 10 and 11. How do you think the kangaroo feels about having possum babies on her tail?
- Look at page 14. How do you think the possum mother felt about having all her babies back?

EXPLORING LANGUAGE

Terminology

Title, cover, illustrations, author, illustrator

Vocabulary

Interest words: possum, pouch, scared, stomach, plonk
High-frequency words: couldn't, keep, could, still
Positional words: in, up, off, under, over, on, into, down

Print Conventions

Capital letter for sentence beginnings, periods, commas, exclamation mark, ellipses, possessive apostrophes